My Secret Unicorn
Unicorn
The Magic Spell

My Secret Unicorn
Unicorn
The Magic Spell

Linda Chapman
Illustrated by Biz Hull

Cover Illustration by Andrew Farley

AN
APPLE
PAPERBACK

SCHOLASTIC INC.
New York   Toronto   London   Auckland   Sydney
Mexico City   New Delhi   Hong Kong   Buenos Aires

No part of this publication may be reproduced in whole or in part, or stored
in a retrieval system, or transmitted in any form or by any means, electronic, mechanical,
photocopying, recording, or otherwise, without written permission of the publisher. For
information regarding permission, write to
Working Partners Limited, 1 Albion Place, London W6 OQT, United Kingdom.

ISBN 0-439-60009-X

Text copyright © 2002 by Working Partners Limited.
Illustrations copyright © 2002 by Biz Hull.
Created by Working Partners Ltd.
All rights reserved. Published by Scholastic Inc.,
557 Broadway, New York, NY 10012, by arrangement with Working Partners Limited.
MY SECRET UNICORN is a trademark of Working Partners Limited.
SCHOLASTIC, APPLE PAPERBACKS, and associated logos are trademarks and/or registered
trademarks of Scholastic Inc.

24 23 22 21 20 19 18 17 16 15   18 19 20

Printed in the U.S.A.   40
First Scholastic printing, November 2003

To Peter, for believing in dragons—
and in unicorns

Prologue

Deep in the mountains, mist swirled over a round stone table. A unicorn was standing beside it. With a snort, it lowered its noble head and touched the table's surface with its golden horn.

The table seemed to shiver for a moment. And then its surface began to shine like a mirror.

The unicorn murmured a name.

There was a flash of
purple light and the
mist cleared.

In the mirror,
an image
appeared. It
was of a small
gray pony.

Another

unicorn came up to the table. It gazed at
the gray pony thoughtfully. "So, he is still
looking for the right owner to free his
powers?" it said.

The golden-horned unicorn nodded.
"His last owner was often unkind."

The other unicorn tossed its mane. Its
silvery horn flashed in the light cast by

the mirror. "Surely, somewhere out there there must be someone who is good–hearted enough? Someone who has the imagination to believe in magic?"

"I think there is," the golden–horned unicorn said softly. "Watch. She is coming."

CHAPTER

One

"Where do you want this box, Mom?" Lauren Foster asked, staggering into the kitchen.

Her mom was kneeling on the floor, surrounded by packing cases. "Just put it anywhere you can find a space, honey," she said.

Lauren went over to the kitchen table and put the box on it. Just then, Max, her younger brother, came running in. Hot on his heels was Buddy, their three-month-old Bernese mountain dog.

The puppy came bounding across the floor to say hello — and crashed straight into a stack of dishes that Mrs. Foster had just unpacked. A couple of plates fell off the pile with a horrible clatter.

"Oh, Buddy . . ." Mrs. Foster sighed.

"It's not his fault," Max said. He rushed over to scoop the fluffy black-and-tan puppy into his arms. "He just hasn't gotten the hang of stopping yet."

Mrs. Foster laughed. "Why don't you take Buddy out into the yard?" she suggested. "You can teach him how to use his brakes."

Max and Buddy rushed out again into the April afternoon sunshine.

"Watch out, Max!" Mr. Foster called from the hallway.

Lauren looked over and saw that Max and Buddy had almost run into two moving men on their way out.

Mr. Foster, Lauren's dad, was directing the men, who were carrying furniture in from the moving van.

"What should I do now, Dad?" Lauren asked.

"Coming through!" another moving man shouted, drowning out her dad's reply.

Lauren dodged out of the way as the man marched past, carrying the family computer. Mr. Foster pushed a hand through his curly brown hair. "Maybe you should go and unpack your bedroom, honey." Without giving her a chance to reply, he hurried after the man with the computer. "Please be careful! That's a delicate piece of equipment!"

Lauren grinned. It was a good idea to escape to her room!

It was strange to think that this house — Granger's Farm — was now her home. As she walked upstairs, Lauren thought about her two best friends back in the city, Carly and Anna. What would they be doing now? Maybe they'd be playing board games or eating the homemade pizza that Anna's mom often made. Lauren wondered if they were missing her.

Feeling a little lonely, she walked through the hall to the bedroom at the far end and pushed open the white-painted wooden door. Her new room was small with a sloping ceiling. Sunlight streamed into the room through a little window.

Lauren stepped over the piles of boxes and suitcases and sat down on the window seat to gaze at the view. The towering Blue Ridge Mountains in the distance were majestic and beautiful, but her eyes passed over them and fell on something much nearer to home: the little paddock and stable behind the house.

As she looked at them, her loneliness lifted. She might not know anyone here in the country but at least she was going to get a pony! A chance to have their

own animals had been the first thing her
parents had promised when they'd told
her and Max about moving from the city.
Mr. Foster had decided to follow his
dream of becoming a farmer. Max had
chosen to have a puppy. They'd gotten
Buddy a couple of weeks ago, and he was
already a big part of the family. Everyone
loved him. But for as long as Lauren
could remember, she had wanted a pony
of her own. And her mom was taking her
to a horse and pony sale the very next
day!

Lauren tried to imagine her pony.
What color would it be? How big? How
old? Maybe it would be a black pony
with four white socks, or a flashy

chestnut, or a snow-white pony with a flowing mane and tail. Lauren smiled to herself. Yes, that's what she'd like — a beautiful white pony.

"Lauren!"

Lauren's eyes shot open. It was her mom, calling from the stairs. Lauren went to the door.

"I've unpacked some cookies," her mom said. "Why don't you come and have some with Max?"

"OK," Lauren replied. And she went back down to join her family.

By the time Lauren went to bed that night, her bedroom was beginning to look more as if it belonged to her. Her clothes were hanging up in the closet, and she had unpacked her books and stuffed animals.

Mrs. Foster gently smoothed Lauren's hair. "Time to get some sleep."

Suddenly, Lauren didn't want to be left alone. This was the first night in their new home and it felt a little strange. "Will you read me a story, Mom?" she asked. Now that she was nine she didn't usually have a bedtime story. But this was an unusual night.

Her mom seemed to understand. "Of course, honey," she said. "Which one do you want?" She looked at the bookshelf.

"*The Little Pony*," Lauren said, snuggling down beneath the blanket. *The*

Little Pony was her favorite story. Mrs. Foster was a writer, and she'd written the story especially for Lauren when Lauren was just three years old. It was about a little white pony who traveled the world trying to find a home. He had almost given up when, one day, he met a girl who became his friend. And from then on, they'd looked after each other.

Her mom sat down on the bed and opened the book. As always, she started at the very first page. *"To Lauren, my very own little girl,"* she read aloud softly. And then she started the story. *"Once upon a time, there was a little white pony that wanted a home. . . ."*

Lauren shut her eyes and smiled at the

familiar, comforting words of the story. Halfway between wakefulness and sleep, plans for the next day swirled in her head. They were going to a horse and pony sale! *This time tomorrow,* she thought, *I'll have a pony of my own!*

CHAPTER

Two

Soon after breakfast, Lauren set off with her mother for the sale. They left Max and her father at home with Buddy.

Even though it was raining, the parking lot was already very busy when they arrived. Horses were being led around, and the air was filled with shouts and whinnies. Loose dogs darted in between people's legs. Stable hands ran around with grooming brushes and saddles.

Lauren felt very excited. "Where do we go?" she asked.

Her mom pointed out a sign that read LIVESTOCK. "The horses and ponies will be over there. The bidding should have just started."

Lauren followed her mom through the crowds until they came to a large covered ring.

A bay horse was being trotted around the ring by a stable hand. A man standing on a platform at one end was calling out a price, raising his voice above the noise of the rain drumming on the roof. "I have a bid of twelve hundred dollars. Do I hear thirteen hundred?"

A woman near Lauren held up her hand.

The man nodded at her. "Thirteen hundred to the lady on my left. Do I hear fourteen hundred dollars?"

Lauren turned to her mom. "So the person who offers the most money gets the horse?"

Her mom nodded. "The auctioneer — that's the man on the platform — keeps raising the price until no one else bids."

"Anyone for fourteen hundred?" the auctioneer shouted. No one moved. He raised a small wooden hammer. "Going, going — gone!" he said, bringing the hammer down on the table beside him with a bang. "Sold to the lady on my left."

The lady smiled and the horse was led out of the ring. A new horse — a big dapple gray — was brought in by another stable hand.

"Come on, let's go look around," Mrs. Foster said to Lauren. She led the way toward an enormous barn beside the ring. Lauren gasped when she looked inside. It was full of pens and nearly all had horses standing in them. There were bays and chestnuts and grays, each awaiting its turn in the ring. Lauren thought they all looked very big.

Lauren's mother had disappeared ahead

of her through a gate, but Lauren didn't want to walk too quickly; she didn't want to miss a thing. Carefully, she avoided the puddles underfoot and made her way through the crowd. She reached the gate at the same time as an elderly lady who was holding a brightly colored umbrella. Lauren held the gate open for her.

The lady nodded. "Thank you," she said.

Lauren followed her through. The lady suddenly slipped on the wet ground and almost fell. "Careful!" Lauren cried. She reached forward to hold the lady's elbow until she had regained her balance.

"Thank you again," the lady said, her face creasing into a wide smile. She had

the friendliest blue eyes that Lauren had
ever seen.

"You're welcome," Lauren said,
smiling. "I'm Lauren," she went on.

"Hello, Lauren," the lady answered.
"So if you're here at the sale, I guess you
like ponies."

Lauren nodded. "I love them! My parents are going to buy me one." She didn't want to sound spoiled, but she couldn't stop herself from blurting out her amazing news.

"Aren't you lucky?" The lady's eyes twinkled as they met Lauren's.

"I'm the luckiest person in the world," Lauren exclaimed. "Will you be OK now? I ought to get going. My mother will be wondering where I am."

"I'll be just fine, thank you," the lady replied. "I hope you find the pony you're looking for."

"Thank you," Lauren said. She scanned the crowds anxiously for her mother. Spotting her, she looked back to say good-bye to the lady, but she had already slipped away.

Lauren shrugged and quickly made her way into the barn, past the horses. As she rounded the corner, she saw her mom ahead of her, at the end of the barn. She was standing beside a row of about ten ponies. Lauren ran to her.

"There you are, Lauren!" her mother exclaimed. "I thought I'd lost you."

"Not a chance." Lauren grinned. She looked excitedly at the ponies in front of her.

In the first pen, there was a tiny black pony. The next pen was empty, but beside it there were two pretty chestnuts with matching white stars on their foreheads.

Next to them was an old gray mare with feathery legs and a large head, and beside her was a mischievous-looking bay. On the door of each pen, there was a card with details about the pony inside.

There was no sparkling white pony like Lauren had been imagining, but she didn't care. "They're all lovely!" she gasped, turning around to her mom.

"Well, this one's much too small," Mrs. Foster said as she looked at the little black pony. "We want a pony that's about thirteen hands high and at least six years old. Any younger and he'll be too inexperienced."

Lauren ran over to the bay gelding's pen and looked at the card attached to his gate. *"Topper,"* she read aloud. *"Thirteen hands. Four years old."* She felt a flicker of disappointment. He was too young. She patted him and moved on.

The gray mare was too tall, the black pony was too small, and the chestnut ponies were only three years old. Lauren walked along the line of ponies, reading their sale notices. She reached the end of the row. Not one of them was right.

Her mom came up behind her and squeezed her shoulder. "Maybe we won't find your perfect pony today. We can always come to the next sale. It's only a month away."

A month! Lauren looked around. She couldn't wait that long. "The little black pony isn't that small," she began desperately. "And he's really cute. . . ."

Just then, she heard the sound of hooves. She swung around. A man was leading a scruffy gray pony out of the vet's tent and down the walkway toward the last empty pen.

"I thought I wasn't going to get here in time for the sale," he said, noticing Lauren and her mom.

The pony looked quiet and sad.

"Hi, boy," Lauren said, going over to him.

At the sound of her voice, the pony lifted his head and pricked his ears. He whinnied, and Lauren felt her heart flip. Suddenly, she didn't care that he was scruffy and dirty. This was the pony she wanted. "How old is he?" she asked the pony's owner.

"Twilight? He's seven," the man replied.

Lauren swung around to her mom. "He's the right age!" The pony stepped forward and thrust his nose into her hands. His breath was warm as he nuzzled at her fingers.

"Can we buy him?" Lauren asked her mother eagerly.

The man smiled at them. "Are you looking for a pony?"

"Yes, we are," Mrs. Foster replied. She walked forward and looked at Twilight. "Why's he for sale, Mr. —?"

"Roberts — Cliff Roberts," the man said, introducing himself and shaking hands. "The pony's for sale because my daughter, Jade, doesn't want him anymore," he explained. "I only bought Twilight for her a few months ago but she says he's too quiet and not showy enough. I've just bought her a new pony to take to shows, so now I've got to sell Twilight."

"Can we buy him?" Lauren asked her mom again.

"Well, you'll have to ride him first," her mom said. She turned to Twilight's owner. "Would that be possible, Mr. Roberts?"

Mr. Roberts smiled. "Of course. It

looks like the rain has stopped now. I'll just go and get the saddle."

Five minutes later, Lauren found herself riding Twilight around the exercise paddock. He felt wonderful. The slightest squeeze of her legs made him go faster and the smallest pull on the reins slowed him down. It was almost as though he could read her mind.

"That's amazing!" Mr. Roberts said as Lauren brought Twilight to a halt by the paddock gate and dismounted. "He hardly wanted to do anything for Jade. He must like you."

"I love him!" Lauren said, her eyes shining. She stretched out her hands

toward Twilight. The pony lowered his
muzzle and blew softly on Lauren's face.
"Please can we buy him?" she begged her
mother. "He's perfect!"

"He certainly seems very well behaved," Mrs. Foster said, patting Twilight. "Maybe we'll bid for him when he goes into the ring."

Lauren thought about the sale and the way the person who offered the most money got the pony. "But someone else might bid more than us," she said in alarm. "Can't we just buy him now?"

"I'm quite happy to arrange a private sale, if you're interested," Mr. Roberts said to Lauren's mother. "I wouldn't have to pay the auction fee then, so it would save me some money. How about we say . . ." He thought for a moment and then named a price. "I'll even throw in the saddle and bridle, if you like."

Lauren looked at her mom and crossed her fingers. She didn't think she could bear to see Twilight go into the ring and be sold to someone else. *Oh, please*, she prayed. *Please say yes.*

To her amazement, her mom smiled. "OK, Mr. Roberts. You've got yourself a deal."

Lauren could hardly believe it. She threw her arms around Twilight's neck and hugged him. "Oh, Twilight!" she gasped in delight. "You're going to be mine!"

The little gray pony nuzzled her happily, as if he understood.

CHAPTER

Three

It was soon arranged that Mr. Roberts would drive Twilight to Granger's Farm the next morning.

"That gives us time to buy everything we need and get the paddock and stable ready," Mrs. Foster said to Lauren.

On the way home, Lauren and her mom drove to the local tack store on the outskirts of town.

The sales assistant, a girl named Jenny, was very helpful. Soon there were lots of horsey things on the counter — brushes, a first-aid kit, feed buckets, a halter. The pile grew bigger and bigger until, at last, Lauren had everything she needed.

Jenny helped them put all their purchases into their car. "Have fun with your new pony!" she called to Lauren.

Lauren grinned at her. "Thanks! I will!"

As Jenny went back into the store, Lauren noticed a small bookstore tucked between the tack store and a store selling electronics. It had an old-fashioned brown-and-gold sign over the window that read MRS. FONTANA'S NEW AND USED

BOOKS. "Look at that bookstore, Mom," she said.

"Do you want to take a look inside?" Mrs. Foster asked.

Lauren nodded eagerly. Both she and her mom loved bookstores, and this one looked really interesting.

They walked along the sidewalk. Through the glass panel in the door, Lauren could see a cheerful rose-patterned carpet and shelves and shelves of books.

Mrs. Foster pushed the door open. A bell jingled, and they stepped inside.

"Wow!" Lauren said, looking around. There were books everywhere! Old books, new books — and not just on the shelves. There were piles of books next to the shelves. And more piles in front of those! But enough space had been left for a few chairs to be placed around a pretty iron fireplace. A large notice said: PLEASE FEEL FREE TO BROWSE AND SIT A WHILE. It was the strangest, loveliest bookstore that Lauren had ever been in.

Just then, there was a pattering of feet, and a little white terrier with a black patch over one eye came trotting up to them. "Look, Mom!" Lauren exclaimed. She crouched down and the terrier licked her hand.

Mrs. Foster bent down to pet him. "Hi, little one," she said.

"Isn't he cute?" said Lauren.

"Ah, I see you've met Walter."

Lauren and her mom looked up. An
elderly lady was coming toward them.
She was wearing an embroidered shawl
over a flowery dress. Lauren gasped. It was
the lady she'd met at the horse sale
earlier! There was no mistaking the warm
blue eyes.

"Hello, Lauren," the lady said, smiling.

"You two know each other?" Lauren's
mother said, looking surprised.

"We met at the horse and pony sale
this morning," the lady explained. She
held out her hand. "I'm Mrs. Fontana,"
she said. "This is my store."

"Alice Foster," Lauren's mom said,
shaking hands. "We've just moved into

the area. Is it OK if we have a look around?"

"Feel free," Mrs. Fontana replied. She smiled at Lauren. "There are lots of books in the side room you might like."

Leaving her mom to browse, Lauren made her way to the side of the store. The next room was full of children's books. There were no bright posters or colorful displays like there were in most bookstores, but there were lots of plump, soft cushions on the floor and a big table piled high with all kinds of books.

Lauren examined each pile and quickly picked out a collection of pony stories. She sat down on one of the cushions and started to read.

Suddenly, she heard the patter of paws coming toward her. It was Walter, the terrier. He sat down beside Lauren and looked at her, his head cocked to one side. Lauren scratched him under the chin.

"He likes you," Mrs. Fontana said.

Lauren jumped. The bookstore owner seemed to have appeared out of nowhere.

She smiled again at Lauren. "So what have you chosen, my dear?"

Feeling slightly shy, Lauren showed Mrs. Fontana the book of pony stories.

"I thought you might like those," Mrs. Fontana said, raising her bright eyes to Lauren's face. "Did you find your pony today?"

"I certainly did," Lauren said, nodding excitedly. "He's coming tomorrow. His name is Twilight and he's wonderful!"

Mrs. Fontana stared at her for a moment and then she swung around. "You know what?" she said. "I think I might have just the thing for you. It's up here."

Lauren watched as Mrs. Fontana got a folding stepladder and stood on it to reach the top shelf. "Here we are," she said, pulling out a dusty purple book. She climbed down the ladder and handed the book to Lauren.

Lauren looked down at the heavy leather volume. It had beautiful gold writing on the cover. Lauren looked at the words. *"The Life of a Unicorn,"* she read aloud.

She opened the book. The pages were smooth and yellowed with age. There was lots of writing, but also some beautiful pictures. Unicorns cantered in the sky and grazed on soft grass. "They're lovely," she said as she turned the pages.

"Yes," Mrs. Fontana agreed, sighing.

Lauren stopped at the next picture. There was no unicorn to be seen, just a small gray pony.

"That's a young unicorn," Mrs. Fontana said, looking over her shoulder.

"But it hasn't got a horn," Lauren said.

"Ah, but, you see, young unicorns don't have horns," Mrs. Fontana told her. "They only grow their horns and receive their magical powers when they hear some magic words. Then they turn into the creatures that we know as unicorns."

Lauren looked at her in surprise. From the way Mrs. Fontana was talking, she made it sound as if unicorns were real.

"But unicorns don't really exist, do they?" Lauren said to her. "They're just made up, like fairies and dragons and trolls."

"You don't think fairies, dragons, and trolls exist, either?" Mrs. Fontana said, raising her eyebrows.

"No way." Lauren grinned.

"Why not?" Mrs. Fontana said.

Looking into Mrs. Fontana's blue eyes, Lauren suddenly felt less certain. "Well, no one has ever seen them," she faltered.

"Maybe that's because they don't *want* to be seen," Mrs. Fontana said. She looked around and then leaned forward. "Can I tell you a secret? I've seen a unicorn."

Lauren stared at her in astonishment. Was Mrs. Fontana crazy?

Mrs. Fontana seemed to read her mind. "Oh, I'm not crazy, dear," she said with a smile. "All that is needed are the magic words, spoken by the right person, a handful of the secret flowers — and a unicorn, of course."

Just then, there was the sound of footsteps. "Are you ready, honey?" Mrs. Foster asked. "We should be going home."

Mrs. Fontana stood up briskly. Lauren felt as if she had been jerked out of a dream.

"What's that?" her mom said, seeing the book in Lauren's hands.

"A . . . a book on unicorns," Lauren said, standing up.

Mrs. Foster glanced at the book. She took in the soft leather binding and the pictures glowing in jewel colors. "It looks very expensive, honey. I'm afraid we can't afford it," she said.

Lauren nodded. She hadn't really expected her mom to buy it for her.

"I'd like you to have it," Mrs. Fontana said softly.

Lauren looked at her in amazement.

The bookstore owner smiled. "Think of it as a gift to welcome you to town."

"But, Mrs. Fontana, that's much too generous. . . ." Mrs. Foster began.

"Not at all," said Mrs. Fontana. "It's a

very special book and it needs a good home. Something tells me that Lauren will look after it."

"Oh, I will!" Lauren gasped. "Thank you, Mrs. Fontana." She took the book in her hands and held it close to her.

The bookstore owner walked with them to the door. "Do come again," she said. "And good luck at Granger's Farm."

"We will — and thank you so much for the welcome gift," Mrs. Foster said.

The door jingled shut behind them. Lauren was suddenly struck by a thought. "How did Mrs. Fontana know that we had moved to Granger's Farm? We didn't tell her."

Mrs. Foster frowned. "Didn't we?"

"No," Lauren said.

Her mom shrugged. "Oh, well, it's a small town. News has probably gotten around. Now, come on. Dad and Max will be wondering where we are."

They got into the car. As her mom

started the engine, Lauren looked back once more at the bookstore. Walter, the little dog, was sitting in the window, staring out. It looked just as if he was smiling at them.

CHAPTER

Four

As Mrs. Foster drove back to Granger's Farm, Lauren looked at the beautiful book she had been given. When she came to the page with the picture of the baby unicorn, she could almost hear Mrs. Fontana's voice saying, *I've seen a unicorn.*

Lauren gently stroked the picture with her fingertip. She was sure that Mrs.

Fontana must have been making up all that stuff about magical creatures. The bookstore owner couldn't really have seen a unicorn.

Could she?

Of course she couldn't, Lauren told herself firmly. *Unicorns don't exist. Mrs. Fontana has just been reading one too many of her old books.*

"So, what did you buy?" Mr. Foster asked, coming out to meet them as they pulled up at the farm. Max ran out after him.

"Lots," Lauren said, jumping out of the car.

"Can I see?" said Max, opening the back door. He pulled a hoof pick out of one of the bags. "What's this for?"

"Come on, Max," Mr. Foster said. "Lauren can explain while we unload."

They carried the bags to the stable, and then Mrs. Foster went into the house to do some more unpacking while Lauren, her dad, and Max carried the purchases for Twilight into the little shed that was going to be his tack room. Mr. Foster hammered two metal hooks into the wall, one for Twilight's bridle and one for his new red-and-blue halter. Then he got a low table and an old striped rug from the garage.

With the rug on the floor, a lightbulb gleaming brightly, and Lauren's shiny new grooming kit and first-aid box laid out on the table, the tack room looked very cozy and cheerful.

"This is great," Lauren said, looking around happily.

"Now all we need is Twilight," Mr. Foster said, smiling at Lauren.

Lauren imagined Twilight's gray head looking out over the stable door. "I can't wait till tomorrow!" she said.

That night, when Lauren went to bed, she opened the book that Mrs. Fontana had given her and began to read the first chapter. "*Noah and the unicorns,*" she whispered quietly to herself. . . .

Many years ago, there was a great flood that threatened both animals and magical creatures. The magical creatures fled to safety in Arcadia, an enchanted land that can't be found by humans.

Meanwhile, a man named Noah gathered together two of every animal and took them onto the Ark he had built. As the rain started to fall, Noah saw two small gray ponies in the grassy meadows beside the rising sea. He took them onto his Ark with the rest of the animals.

Through a magic mirror, the unicorns in Arcadia watched gratefully as Noah took care of their young. For these two gray ponies were, in fact, baby unicorns who hadn't yet grown into their magical powers. They had been left behind in the rush to Arcadia.

While on the Ark, the time for the two

young unicorns to gain their magical powers
came and went. They had lost their chance.
And the unicorns in Arcadia mourned.

When a whole year had passed, the floods
went down. Noah released the young unicorns
onto the earth with the other animals. And
there they remained, trapped in their pony
bodies.

Back in Arcadia, the watching unicorns
worked on a Turning Spell that would give the
unicorns another chance to gain their magical
powers. The spell took years and years to
perfect. At last it was ready. But the spell
would only free a unicorn if spoken by a good-
hearted human who believed in magic.

A very brave unicorn risked his own powers
to fly back to Earth. He searched long and

hard for a human to whom he could entrust the spell. Eventually, he found her.

The spell worked — and the two young unicorns became great friends with the human who had helped them. They grew beautiful horns and flew like angels. And together they had many magical adventures. . . .

CHAPTER

Five

Lauren put the book down. The way the book was written made everything about unicorns sound so real, not like a made-up story at all. She looked at the picture at the end of the chapter. It showed a beautiful unicorn cantering up into the sky.

I wish the story were true, Lauren

thought. *I wish there were still unicorns on Earth. I'd love to help one.*

And then she smiled. Unicorns might not exist, but Twilight did, and he was going to arrive the very next day.

Mr. Roberts arrived with Twilight at ten o'clock. He opened the side door of the trailer so that Lauren could get inside. Twilight whinnied as she stepped into the trailer.

"Hello, little one," Lauren said, stroking his nose.

Twilight looked at her. *Hello,* his dark eyes seemed to say back.

Mr. Roberts lowered the ramp to the

ground. "You can bring him out now, Lauren!" he called.

Lauren untied Twilight and backed carefully out of the trailer. Her mom and dad and Max came over.

"Hello, boy," Mrs. Foster said, feeding Twilight a carrot.

"He's really dirty, isn't he?" Max said as he patted Twilight and a cloud of dust flew into the air.

Twilight whinnied indignantly, as if he understood what Max had said.

Mr. Roberts smiled ruefully. "I'm afraid my daughter has been busy with her new pony. She hasn't been looking after Twilight as well as she should." He looked at Lauren. "You'd like Jade. She's just crazy about ponies."

Lauren wasn't so sure. If Mr. Roberts's daughter was really crazy about ponies, she would have looked after Twilight better. But she didn't say anything.

While Mr. and Mrs. Foster paid Mr. Roberts, Lauren and Max led Twilight to his stable.

"Are you going to ride now, Lauren?" Max asked.

"I'm going to groom him first," Lauren replied.

She tied Twilight up outside the stable and got the grooming kit.

"Can I help?" asked Max.

"OK," Lauren said, handing him a brush with thick bristles called a dandy brush. It was good for getting rid of dirt and dust. "You can brush him with that."

Twilight nuzzled her shoulder. Lauren smiled happily and kissed his face. She didn't think she'd ever felt happier in her life.

Two hours later, Twilight was looking much better. Lauren and Max had brushed him and washed his mane and tail. Instead of being a dirty gray color, he was now pale gray. The dust had come out of his coat, and Lauren had replaced the old ratty halter he had been wearing

with the new red–and–blue one that she
and her mom had bought the day before.
However, despite everything, Twilight
still looked a bit scruffy. His coat didn't

really shine, and the long hair around his hooves and under his chin was quite straggly. Still, Lauren didn't mind.

With her mom's help, Lauren tacked Twilight up and rode him into the paddock. Just like the day before, he seemed to know exactly what she wanted him to do, and soon they were cantering around the field. When Lauren finally stopped him by the gate, her face was flushed and her eyes were shining.

"He's just great!" she said to her mom, who was watching with Max. "Can I go for a ride in the woods?" She saw her mom look doubtful. "I won't go far."

"OK," Mrs. Foster agreed. "But don't stay out too long."

"I won't. I promise," Lauren said. She
remounted and rode Twilight out of the
paddock. The mountain that rose up
behind the farmhouse was thickly
wooded and, as she rode Twilight into
the trees, she felt his ears prick and his
step quicken.

Lauren smiled happily. "You like it up
here, don't you, boy?"

Twilight snorted and broke into a trot.

Lauren let him have his way and he
broke into a canter. They made their way
along the trail. The air was so still that the
only sound, apart from the thudding of
Twilight's hooves on the soft ground, was
the distant calling of birds in the tops of

the trees. Lauren felt that she could have gone on forever. But she remembered what she had promised her mom, so she slowed Twilight down to turn him around.

Twilight looked to one side. A small side trail led off the main track. He pulled toward it. Lauren stopped him. "No," she told him. "We've got to go back now." Twilight pulled toward the side trail again.

"We'll go another day," Lauren told him and then, turning him around, she rode back to the farm.

That night, when Lauren went to bed, she opened the unicorn book to a

beautiful picture showing unicorns
grazing in lush meadows dotted with star-
shaped purple flowers. The pink sky was
streaked with orange and gold, as if the
sun was setting. She began to read. . . .

When the two young unicorns grew old, they
returned to Arcadia. The unicorn elders
decided that from then on they would send
young unicorns to Earth to do good works.
They look like small ponies. Each of them
hopes to find someone who will learn how to
free their magical powers. To do this, one needs
the words of the Turning Spell, a hair from the
unicorn's mane, the petals from a single
moonflower, and the light of the Twilight Star,
which only shines for ten minutes after the sun
has set.

Lauren turned the page and saw the
picture of the young unicorn that she had
seen in Mrs. Fontana's store. Scruffy and
gray, it looked a lot like Twilight.

Maybe Twilight's a unicorn in disguise, Lauren thought suddenly.

She smiled to herself. She was being silly. It was just a made-up story and Twilight was just a regular pony.

CHAPTER

Six

After breakfast the next morning, Lauren took Twilight out for a ride in the woods again. It felt a little lonely on her own. *I wish I had someone else to ride with,* she thought. She wondered if she would make friends with someone when school started.

As they reached the trees, Twilight

pricked up his ears and pulled at the reins.

"OK, boy," Lauren said, letting him trot.

She had been riding for ten minutes when Twilight suddenly stopped.

"Go on!" Lauren encouraged him.

But Twilight wouldn't move. He shook his head and looked to the left.

Lauren realized that he was looking along the same side trail he had tried to go down the last time they had been in the woods. She thought for a moment. What harm could there be in exploring?

"All right," she said, turning Twilight toward it.

The trail was narrow and the trees on

either side met over Lauren's head, blocking out the sun. It was like riding through a long, green tunnel. As the silence closed in around them, Lauren began to wonder where the trail was leading.

"Maybe we should turn back," she whispered to Twilight, but the pony pulled eagerly on the reins. It was clear he didn't want to stop.

Lauren saw light ahead. It looked as if the trail was coming to an end. Wondering where they would come out, she let Twilight continue on. He trotted out from among the trees and into a grassy glade.

It was beautiful. In the center of the

glade, there was a mound dotted with purple flowers, where a cloud of yellow butterflies fluttered in the sunlight.

Twilight walked to the mound, and
Lauren saw that the flowers were star-
shaped with a golden spot at the tip of

each bright petal. She frowned. She knew she had seen them somewhere before, but she couldn't remember where.

With a soft whicker, Twilight bent his head. Thinking he was grabbing a mouthful of grass, Lauren tried to pull his head up. "No, Twilight!"

But as she spoke she realized that he wasn't eating, he was nuzzling at the star-shaped flowers. Her curiosity was sparked, and she dismounted.

Looping the reins around her arm, she looked closely at the flowers. Where had she seen them before?

Twilight whickered and nudged her arm. Lauren was puzzled. *It's as if he is trying to tell me something,* she thought, then she shook her head. *He's just a pony*, she reminded herself quickly.

She glanced around. The glade was so beautiful and peaceful that she didn't want to leave. But she knew that she ought to be getting home, so she mounted Twilight and rode him back into the trees.

Lauren turned Twilight onto the main trail through the woods where the birds were singing overhead again. Leaning forward, she let him go faster, and they cantered along the trail toward home.

When they got back to the farm, Lauren went into the study, where her dad had lots of books about plants. She took the

biggest one down from the shelf and
began to look through the section on
woodland flowers. There were quite a
few plants with purple flowers, but none
of them was star-shaped with golden
spots on the edge of the petals. She tried
another book and then another. But she
couldn't find any flowers that looked like
the ones in the glade.

She closed the last book and sighed.
She knew she had seen the flowers
somewhere before.

"I thought I heard you in here," Mrs.
Foster said, coming into the study. "What
are you doing?"

"I've been trying to find the name of
some flowers I saw in the woods," Lauren

replied. She wondered if her mom would know what they were. "They were purple, sort of star-shaped with a gold spot at the tip of each petal."

"Sorry, I can't help you," her mom said. "They sound very unusual, though. Now," she went on, changing the subject, "we need to get you some things for school — you start next week. Why don't you run upstairs and get changed and we'll go to the mall?"

"OK," Lauren said.

She hurried up to her room and pulled on a pair of clean jeans and a sweatshirt. The unicorn book was lying on her bedside table. It was still open at the picture of the unicorns grazing. As

Lauren zipped up her jeans, she glanced at it again: the unicorns, the grassy meadows, the purple flowers . . .

The purple flowers!

She stared at the picture. They were exactly the same as the ones she had just seen in the woods!

CHAPTER

Seven

Lauren snatched up the book. The flowers in the picture had the same star shape, the same gold spot. A wild thought filled her mind. The book had said that unicorns disguised as ponies could be changed back by saying a magic spell and using a certain type of flower. What if the flowers she had found in the woods were the very ones that were needed in the spell?

She quickly turned the pages of the book until she found the part that explained how unicorns disguised as ponies could be changed back into unicorns. In the middle of the page, there was a small picture of a purple flower just like the ones in the wood. Lauren read the words under the picture.

The moonflower: a rare, purple-flowering herb that is used in the Turning Spell.

Lauren stared. She'd found the flower that the book said could give a unicorn its magical powers. She remembered the way

Twilight had been nuzzling at the flowers
in the glade. Maybe the story was true . . .
and maybe, just maybe, Twilight really
was a unicorn in disguise!

    Her heart started to race. If she could

just find the words of the spell, then she could try it out.

"Lauren! Are you coming?" her mom called.

Lauren could hardly bear to put the book down. The spell had to be here somewhere.

"Lauren!" her mom called again.

Lauren closed the book reluctantly. "I'm coming!" she called, and she went downstairs.

Normally, Lauren loved buying things for a new school year, but not that day. All she could think about was unicorns.

On the way home, Mrs. Foster

stopped by the tack store to pick up a couple of spare feed buckets.

Lauren had an idea. "Can I go and look in the bookstore?" she asked.

"Sure," Mrs. Foster agreed. "I'll meet you there in a few minutes."

Lauren ran to the bookstore. The doorbell jingled as she went inside. The store was just as she remembered it: the piles of books, the rose-patterned carpet. She caught sight of the owner near the back of the store. "Mrs. Fontana!" she called.

The bookstore owner turned around. "Hello, dear," she said. "What can I do for you?"

Suddenly, Lauren didn't know what to say. Mrs. Fontana looked so calm and ordinary that the whole idea of asking her if she knew what the magic spell was seemed really dumb. "Um . . . well . . . I . . ." Lauren stammered.

"So, have you seen a unicorn yet?" Mrs. Fontana said softly.

Lauren stopped stammering and stared.

"That's what you wanted to come in and talk to me about, isn't it?" Mrs. Fontana said.

Lauren didn't even stop to ask how the woman knew. "Is the story really true?" she gasped.

Mrs. Fontana smiled. "It's true for those who want it to be true."

"Do you know what the spell is?" Lauren asked eagerly.

"I do, but I can't tell you," the old lady replied. "Those who want to find unicorns must do it for themselves. You have everything you need."

"But . . ." Lauren began.

Just then, Walter gave a warning bark. The store door swung open, and Lauren's mom came in. "Hello, Mrs. Fontana," she said.

"Hello," the bookstore owner said with a smile. "So how are you settling in at Granger's Farm?" Her tone changed and now she sounded brisk and efficient.

Lauren waited while the two adults chatted. She felt frustrated. If Mrs.

Fontana really knew what the spell was, why wouldn't she tell it to her? She longed to ask the bookstore owner more, but she couldn't with her mom standing there.

Lauren thought about Mrs. Fontana's words: *You have everything you need.*

What did she mean?

That night, when she went to bed, Lauren decided to read the book from the beginning through to the end.

Starting at the first chapter, she began to read slowly and carefully. She read that after the floods had gone down, the magical creatures decided not to live on Earth anymore and stayed in Arcadia.

Arcadia was ruled by seven Golden Unicorns who watched Earth through a magic mirror.

Lauren read on, but she didn't find the spell.

She awoke the following morning to see the book lying beside her on her bed. She had just two chapters left to read. She wondered whether to start them, but then she saw that it was seven o'clock. It was time to get up and give Twilight his breakfast. She took the book outside with her. She could read it while he was eating.

Leaving it in the tack room, she brought Twilight in from the paddock and put him in his stall. Then she mixed his feed. The sooner Twilight was fed, the sooner she could read a little more.

Quickly, Lauren emptied the feed into the manger, and then she got the book. Carrying it into his stable, she sat down on an overturned bucket and began to read. Surely the spell had to be in the book somewhere!

Lauren became aware that Twilight had stopped eating. He was staring at the book. With a snort, he walked over to her.

"Hello, boy," she said.

Twilight blew gently. The pages of the book fluttered over.

"Twilight! You've lost my place!"

Lauren said. But before she could turn
back to the page she had been reading,
Twilight breathed out again.

"What are you doing?" Lauren asked

as he nuzzled his soft lips against the back cover. They left a damp mark on the paper and she started to push his muzzle away but, as she did, she realized that the last page of the book had been glued to the back cover. One corner of the page fluttered slightly as Twilight breathed on the book.

Lauren carefully pulled at it. The glue gave way and the page turned.

Inside the cover were some faint words written in pencil. It looked like a poem of some sort. Lauren read the title: *The Turning Spell*.

CHAPTER

Eight

Trembling with excitement, Lauren read the faintly penciled words:

Twilight Star, Twilight Star,
Twinkling high above so far.
Shining light, shining bright,
Will you grant my wish tonight?
Let my little horse forlorn
Be at last a unicorn!

Her eyes flew to Twilight. "Oh, Twilight," she whispered. "It's the spell!"

Twilight bent his head as if he was nodding.

Lauren jumped to her feet. She had to take Twilight to the woods and pick one of those flowers!

After giving Twilight time to digest his breakfast, Lauren tacked him up and rode into the woods. Twilight seemed to know just where they were going. With his ears pricked up, he cantered along until they came to the little side trail.

They turned down the narrow path and followed it until they reached the sunny glade. It looked just the same as the

day before. A cloud of butterflies
swooped over the grass, and the air had
an expectant feeling.

Lauren dismounted and led Twilight
over to the grassy mound, where she
found a single purple flower that had
fallen to the ground. She picked it up.
As she did so, a sharp tingle ran down her
spine.

She felt Twilight's warm breath on her
shoulder, and she looked at him. "Oh,
Twilight," she whispered. "I hope this is
going to work."

"Dad, what time does the sun set?"
Lauren asked her father that afternoon.
Her book had said that the Twilight Star

only shone for ten minutes after the sun
had set and that the spell had to be
performed then.

"About seven o'clock today," her dad
said. "Why?"

"I just wondered," Lauren said quickly.

At six-thirty, her mom put dinner on the table.

Lauren ate as fast as she could. "May I be excused, please?" she asked as soon as her plate was empty.

Her mom looked surprised. "You know better, Lauren — not till everyone's fnished," she said.

So Lauren had to wait. Through the kitchen window she watched the sun dropping lower and lower in the sky. She was going to miss the sunset!

At long last, her dad put his knife and fork down. "That was delicious," he said.

Before he had even finished speaking, Lauren had jumped to her feet. "May I go and see Twilight now, Mom?" she begged.

"All right," Mrs. Foster said. "Go ahead."

Lauren grabbed her jacket and ran out the door. The book was still in the tack room. She grabbed it and raced down to the paddock. Her heart was pounding in her chest. What would happen? Would the spell really work?

Twilight was standing by the gate. He whinnied when he saw her. Lauren led him toward the far corner of the field. It was shaded by trees and hidden from the house by the stable block.

As soon as they were out of sight of the house, Lauren carefully pulled a single hair out of Twilight's mane, opened the book, and took the flower out of her pocket. The golden spots on the petals seemed to glow in the last rays of the sun.

She looked up. The final curve of the sun was just sinking on the horizon. Lauren's eyes narrowed as she searched for the star. But there was nothing. Maybe she had missed it?

Twilight whickered.

"Ssh, Twilight," Lauren said. She turned and patted his neck. Then she looked back up into the sky and gasped. High above her, a star had appeared. It was time for the spell!

"Please work," Lauren whispered. She took a deep, trembling breath and began to tear the petals off the flower. As she did so, she read the spell aloud.

> *Twilight Star, Twilight Star,*
> *Twinkling high above so far.*
> *Shining light, shining bright,*
> *Will you grant my wish tonight?*
> *Let my little horse forlorn*
> *Be at last a unicorn!*

As she read the last word, she held her breath.

Nothing happened.

Lauren looked down at the petals in her hand and felt a wave of disappointment hit her. It was just a story after all.

She looked at Twilight and felt tears prickle in her eyes. She had so badly wanted him to be a unicorn.

Swallowing hard, she dropped the petals on the ground.

There was a flash of purple light, so bright that it made Lauren shut her eyes. When she opened them again, she gasped.

Twilight had disappeared!

CHAPTER

Nine

Lauren swung around, looking for Twilight. A snow-white unicorn was flying in the sky behind her. Its hooves and horn gleamed silver, and its mane and tail swirled around it.

"Twilight?" Lauren gasped.

"Yes," the unicorn said. "It's me. It feels a bit wobbly up here. This is the first time I've flown. Whoops . . ." He flew down through the air toward Lauren, narrowly missing a low branch. With a kick of his hind legs, he landed on the grass beside her. "Hello," he said, walking over and nuzzling her.

Although Twilight's words rang out clearly in Lauren's head, his mouth didn't move.

"You can talk!" Lauren said in astonishment.

"Only while I'm in my magical shape," Twilight told her. "And you'll only be able to hear me if you're touching me or holding a hair from my mane."

"I can't believe you're really a unicorn!" Lauren exclaimed.

Twilight laughed. "Well, I am. I was

trapped in my pony body, but you freed
me, Lauren, and that means you are my
Unicorn Friend."

"Unicorn Friend?" Lauren echoed.

Twilight nodded his beautiful head.
"Yes. Every unicorn is looking for a
Unicorn Friend to do good deeds with."

"So everything in that book is true?"
Lauren gasped.

"Everything," Twilight replied,
merrily tossing his mane. He knelt down
by bending his forelegs. "Climb on my
back and let's try flying together. You'll
have to excuse me if I'm a bit wobbly."

Lauren took hold of his mane and
mounted. "What if I fall off?"

"You can't fall while I am in my

magical shape," Twilight said. "Unicorn magic will keep you safe."

Lauren grabbed his mane, and he plunged forward into a canter.

"Whoa . . . hold on tight!" Twilight called.

Twilight's hooves skimmed across the grass, and the ground dropped away. "Here we go!" he called to her.

His back legs kicked down powerfully, and with a jolt, they flew up into the air, lurching from side to side.

"Don't worry, I'll get the hang of this soon," Twilight said confidently.

Lauren held on tight. "Wow!" she gasped as she looked down.

Twilight surged upward toward the

stars, and the wind streamed through Lauren's hair as they settled into a steadier pace. "This is amazing!" she cried.

She looked down. Below her she could see her house and the woods.

Suddenly, Lauren caught sight of a figure walking out of the trees. A white terrier dog with a black patch trotted at the person's side. "It's Mrs. Fontana!" she exclaimed.

Mrs. Fontana looked up and raised her hand in greeting. "Hello there!" she called.

Twilight swooped toward her and landed lightly on the soft grass.

Lauren scrambled off Twilight's back. "Mrs. Fontana!" she gasped.

Mrs. Fontana smiled at Lauren. "I see you've found yourself a friend."

Lauren nodded. "Thank you for giving me the book!" she said.

"It was time it had a new owner," Mrs. Fontana replied. "But you must promise to guard the secret carefully. A unicorn's powers can attract bad people who want to use the

magic selfishly. You must not tell a soul.
Do you understand?"

At first, Lauren felt disappointed. She
had been thinking how amazed her mom
and dad would be when she told them.
But she could see the sense in what
Mrs. Fontana was saying. "I understand,"
she said. "And I promise I won't tell
anyone."

"Good," Mrs. Fontana said. "Now,"
she went on, seeming to produce a piece
of paper out of thin air, "I will give you
the Undoing Spell that will turn Twilight
back into a pony. Say it when you return
home."

With that, Mrs. Fontana handed the

paper to Lauren, and Lauren read the
words:

Twilight Star, Twilight Star,
Twinkling high above so far,
Protect this secret from prying eyes
And return my unicorn to his disguise.
His magical shape is for my eyes only,
Let him be once more a pony.

"Keep Twilight's secret, Lauren," Mrs.
Fontana reminded her.

"I will," Lauren promised.

Twilight bent his knees again and
Lauren climbed onto his back. With two
bounds, he cantered across the grass and
rose up into the sky.

"Bye, Mrs. Fontana!" Lauren called, catching hold of Twilight's mane.

Mrs. Fontana raised her hand. "Use the magic well, my dear," she called, and with that, she and Walter disappeared into the dark woods.

Twilight and Lauren flew through the sky. Lauren thought she had never felt happier or more excited. There was so much to see. They flew over the woods and rivers and Mrs. Fontana's bookstore, and finally they flew out over the mountains that rose behind Granger's Farm.

At last they returned to the paddock. As they flew down, Lauren suddenly remembered about her parents.

"Twilight!" she gasped. "I hope Mom and Dad aren't worried about me."

"Don't worry," Twilight told her. "We haven't been gone very long."

"Oh, Twilight," Lauren said, "this is all so exciting!"

Twilight nodded eagerly. "And the excitement's only just beginning. Soon we'll be having all sorts of adventures together." He nuzzled her leg. "Oh, Lauren. I'm so happy you're my Unicorn Friend."

Lauren hugged him. "And I'm so happy you're my unicorn."

As Lauren dismounted, she took the piece of paper that Mrs. Fontana had given her out of her pocket. Slowly, she

read the Undoing Spell aloud. As she
spoke the last word, there was a flash of
blinding purple light and suddenly,
Lauren felt cold air on her face. She
opened her eyes. She was still standing
beside Twilight, but he was no longer a
unicorn; he was just a small gray pony.
For a moment, Lauren wondered if she'd

imagined everything, but then she looked down at the piece of paper in her hand. No, it had been real.

Twilight snuffled at her hair, and she felt a surge of excitement fizz inside her.

"Good night," Lauren whispered, kissing him in delight. Then, picking up the book from the grass, she turned and ran to the house.

As she hurried in, Buddy bounded over to greet her, almost knocking her down in his excitement.

Her dad was washing the dishes at the sink, and her mom was pouring Max a drink of milk.

"How was Twilight?" her mom asked.

"He was fine," Lauren said. "I . . . I

think I'll go up to my room and read for a while."

She went upstairs and sat down by her bedroom window. Twilight was grazing in his paddock. Seeming to sense that Lauren was looking at him, he raised his head and whinnied.

A broad grin crept across Lauren's face.

Her new pony had turned out to be her secret unicorn.

What adventures they were going to have!

Make sure to look for more adventures with Lauren and Twilight in . . .

My Secret Unicorn
Dreams Come True

That evening, Lauren crept out of the house again.

"Are we going to see Shadow?" Twilight asked.

"Yes. Let's be quick," Lauren said, getting onto his back.

As they flew to Goose Creek Farm, she told him what Mrs. Fontana had said. "You have powers that can help," she told him.

"But how can I use them if I don't know what they are?" Twilight said.

"I don't know," Lauren admitted. She'd been thinking the same thing ever since she'd left Mrs. Fontana's shop.

Shadow was waiting for them. He whinnied.

"You were great today, Shadow!" Twilight said as he landed.

Shadow bowed his head, as if a little embarrassed by the praise. He snorted.

"He wants to know if he should try trotting over the poles again," Twilight told Lauren.

"What about trying a small jump?"

Lauren suggested hopefully.

Shadow looked worried.

"Go on, just try," Twilight said.

Shadow hesitated for a moment and then slowly nodded.

Before Shadow could change his mind, Lauren scrambled off Twilight and put up a tiny jump. "You can do it, Shadow!" she said.

Shadow nodded and, turning toward the jump, he began to trot.

"He's going to do it!" Lauren gasped to Twilight.

But then Shadow stopped dead.

"Oh, no." Lauren sighed.

She and Twilight trotted over. Shadow

was standing a few feet away from the jump. "What's wrong?" Lauren asked him. "Why did you stop?"

The dapple-gray pony hung his head and snorted sadly.

"He was just too scared," Twilight told Lauren.

Shadow looked so dejected that Lauren was sure that if ponies could cry, he would have been in tears.

Twilight stepped forward and touched his glowing horn to Shadow's neck. "It's OK," Lauren heard him say softly. "You tried your best. Don't be upset."

They stood there for a moment, and then Lauren saw the little dapple-gray pony's ears flicker forward. He raised his head and whickered in a surprised sort of way.

"What's he saying?" Lauren asked Twilight.

"That he's feeling a little better," Twilight replied.

Shadow whickered again.

"Much better," Twilight said.

Lauren saw Shadow look at the jump. His eyes suddenly seemed to be full of confidence. He whinnied.

"In fact, he says he feels so much better that he thinks he might be able to clear the jump," Twilight said, looking astonished.

Shadow pricked up his ears and trotted away from them. Turning toward the jump, he started to canter. Lauren and Twilight watched in amazement as he flew over it.